Get Set, Georgette!

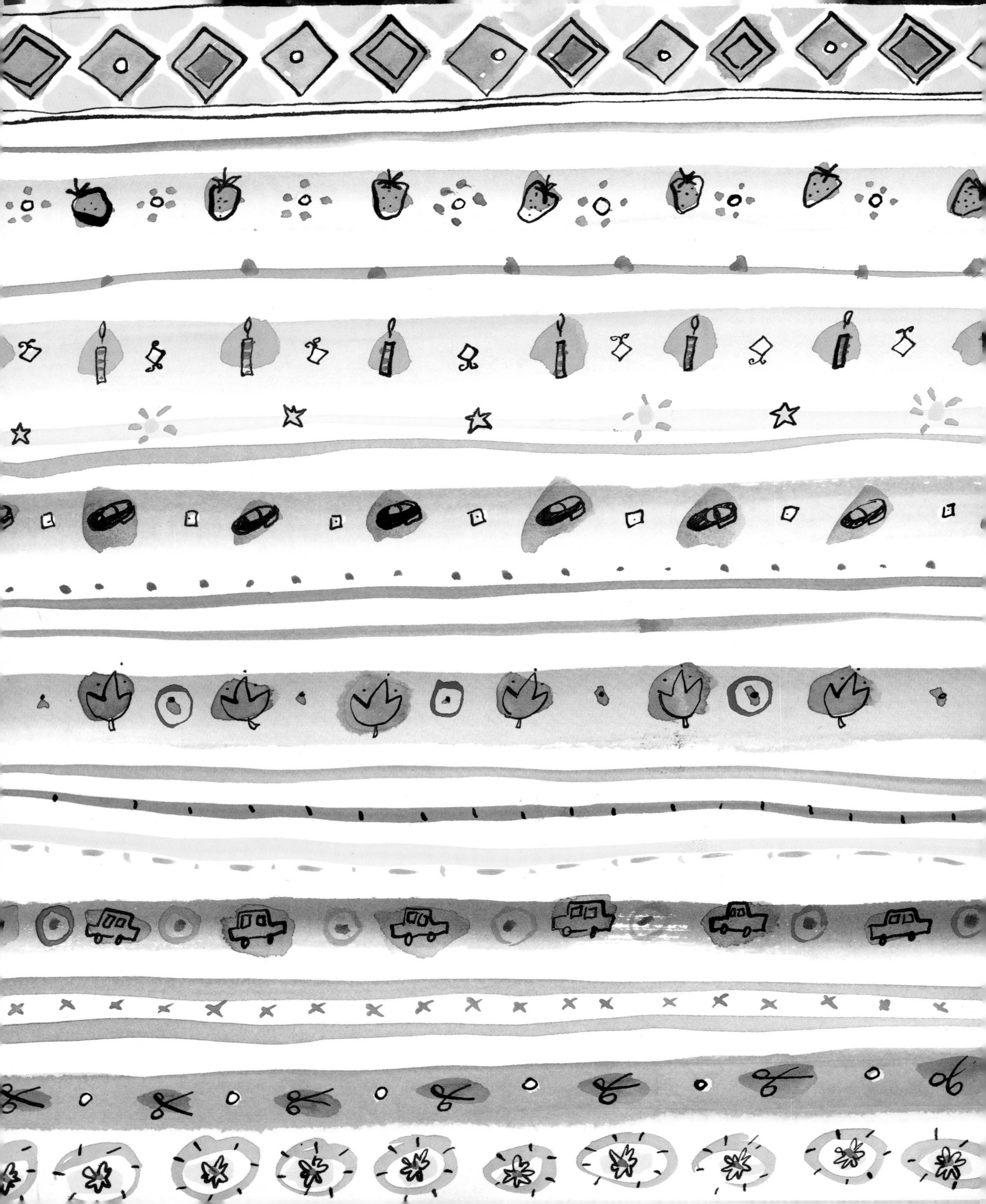

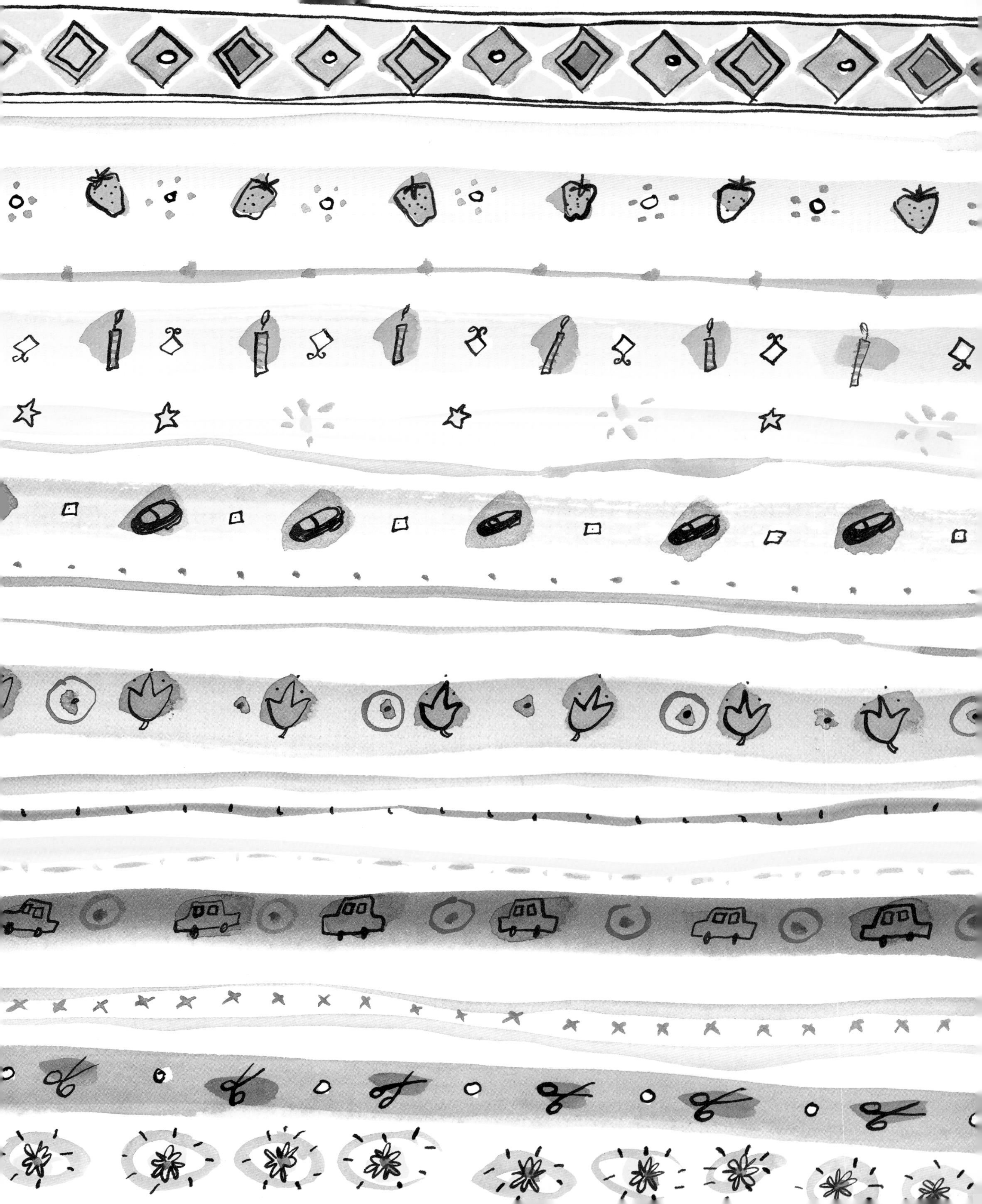

For my parents
who dressed me so well

Also by Alice Dumas

TERESA, OUR AU PAIR

First published 1994 by
Macmillan Children's Books,
Macmillan Publishers Ltd
a division of Macmillan Ltd
Cavaye Place, London SW10 9PG
and Basingstoke
Associated companies throughout the world

This edition first published 1996

1 3 5 7 9 8 6 4 2

ISBN 0 333 63838 7

A CIP catalogue record for this book is
available from the British Library.

Printed in Hong Kong

Get Set, Georgette!

Alice Dumas

MACMILLAN
CHILDREN'S BOOKS

"Now, Georgette, you know it's Rebecca's birthday party today. Daddy and I have got to go out, so let's get you ready now."

"Come along.
You can't go looking
like that."

“Now don’t cry.
There’s absolutely no
soap in your eyes.

A little trim
can only do
your hair good.”

"This is what hairdressers call a blow dry. Isn't it exciting to look different?

There.
That's better, isn't it?
Much neater."

Auntie Gladys, who has been to cake-decorating classes, is making a special cake for Rebecca's party.

"Can I help you, Auntie?"

"No, everything is under control, thank you. You had better go up and put on your frock. Ooh! Your hair does look nice."

“Come and put your dress on, Georgette. This lovely one Grandma made for you last Christmas!”

"Well, aren't you a pretty girl now?

But the trainers won't do . . .
Go and find your party shoes."

"I hate birthday parties
when they are so complicated."

"Did you remember to get a present for Rebecca?"
"Yes, I've got a stick insect for her."
"Oh, Georgette, that won't do at all.

Nancy, take Georgette with Felicity and Isidore to the shops and buy something useful. And do hurry up, children. You know we have to go to Grandma's soon and Georgette must be ready when Mrs. Smith comes to pick her up."

“You know, Georgette, it’s so much nicer to see you in a dress for once.”

“I don’t want to give Rebecca a horrid pink frog.”

"Oh come on, it's sweet.
And a money box is useful.
I'm sure Mummy'll like it."

"Well then. You're all set . . .
Just be a good girl and
watch television until Mrs. Smith
comes to collect you."

"Come on, we have to go!
Mrs. Rose is in the garden,
she'll keep an eye on you."

"Goodbye! Say hello to grandma for me!"
"I'm in the garden if you need me," Mrs. Rose calls out.

"RIGHT!"

"QUICK!"

First let's get rid of those curls . . .

Now brighten up the dress.
I'm sure Grandma will understand.

And a few more glittery bits.

I didn't know Mummy had so many nice hats.

Rover! Felix!
Here's a little present
from Auntie Gladyyyys!

I know Rebecca doesn't like blue icing.
And there's a little bit for Napoleon.

Now let's see . . . Some walnut pieces and whirly candles.

Squeeze cream on top.
That looks much nicer!

I'll put the present away for next Christmas. I know Rebecca would rather have my stick insect.

I wonder if Mummy's shoes will fit me?

Probably not.
But my trainers will do!

That's better than a
boring old money box.

I"ll just make her a card . . .

. . . and pick some
flowers for her Mummy.

Good gracious!

"I'm all ready Mrs. Smith!"

THE END

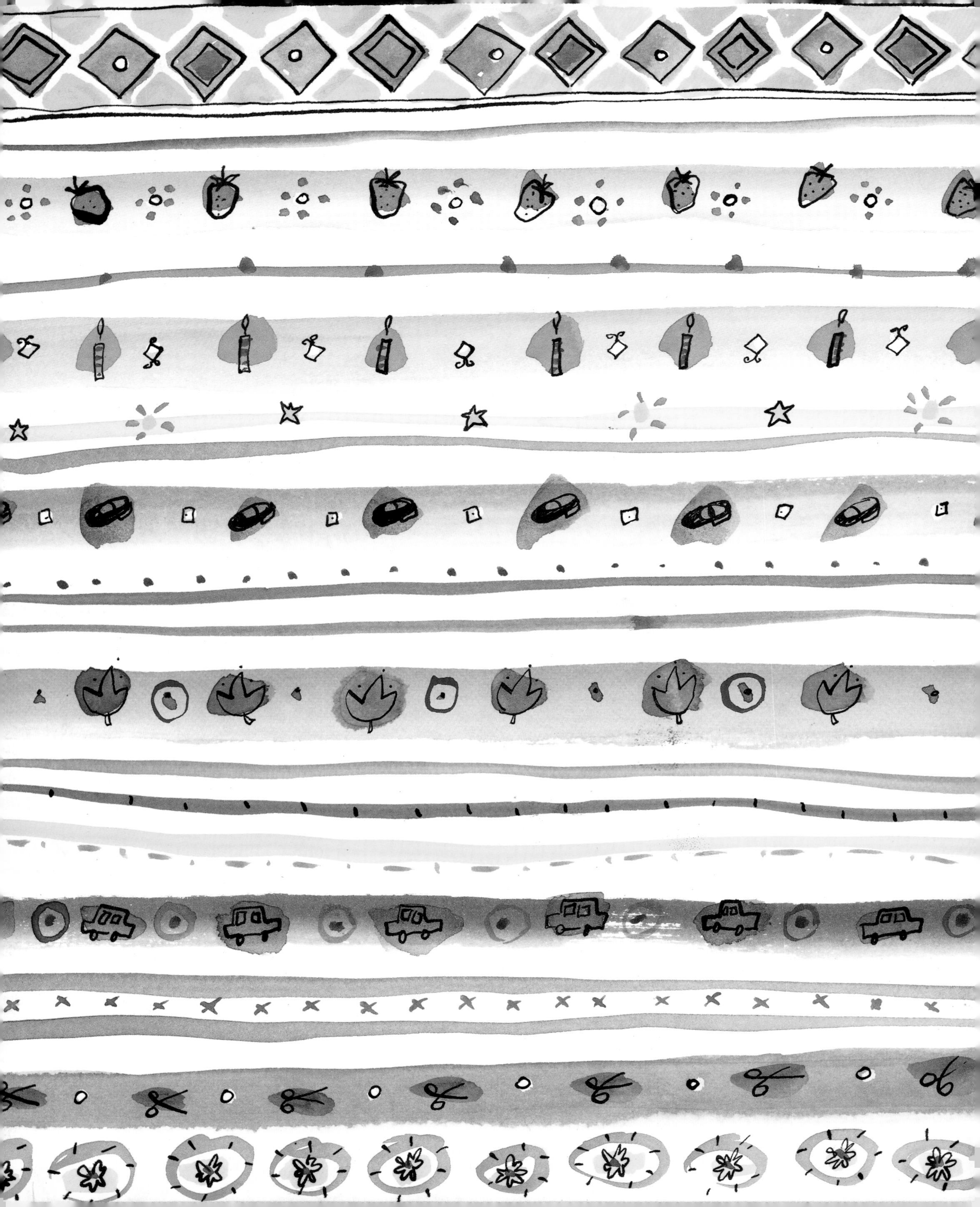

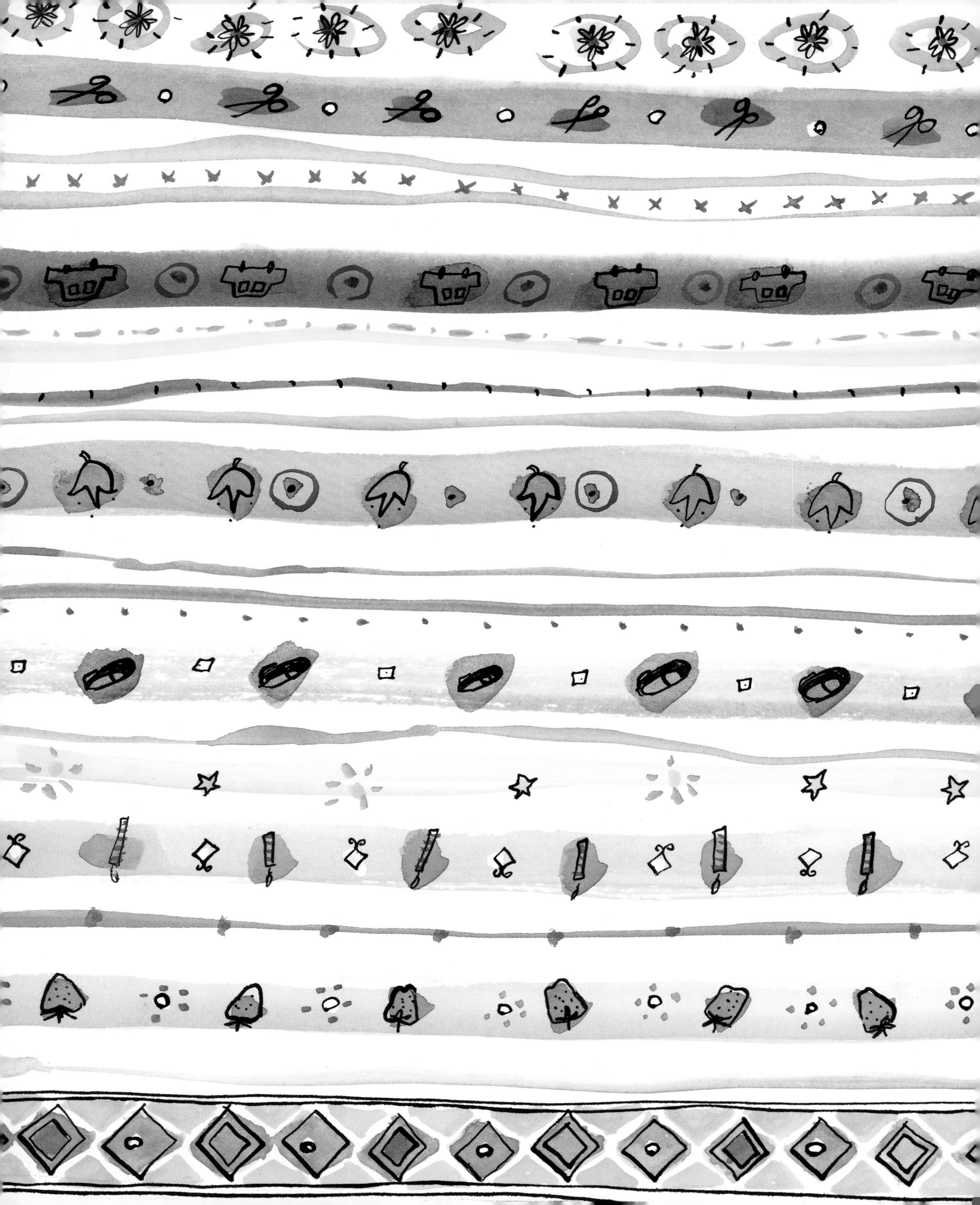